Jasper & Joop

Olivier Dunrea

HOUGHTON MIFFLIN HARCOURT
Boston   New   York

To access the read-along audio file, visit
WWW.HMHBOOKS.COM/FREEDOWNLOADS
ACCESS CODE: PLAY

AGES	GRADES	GUIDED READING LEVEL	READING RECOVERY LEVEL	LEXILE® LEVEL
4-6	1	F	9-10	380L

The text of this book is set in Shannon.
The illustrations are pen-and-ink and gouache on 140-pound d'Arches coldpress watercolor paper.

The Library of Congress Cataloging-in-Publication Data is on file.

ISBN: 978-0-544-50382-3 paper-over-board reader
ISBN: 978-0-544-50381-6 paperback reader

Manufactured in China
SCP 10 9 8 7 6 5 4 3 2 1
4500530678

For my brother, Carl, of course!

This is Jasper.

This is Joop.

Jasper is a small, white gosling
who likes to be tidy.

Joop is a small, gray gosling
who likes to be messy.

Each morning Jasper tidies
his nest and puts on his cap
and tie.

Each morning Joop rumples
his nest and musses his
feathers.

Jasper pokes his head outside.
"It's wet," he says.

Joop pokes his head outside.
"It's WET!" he honks.

Jasper jumps over the puddle.
"Too wet," he says.

Joop splashes into the puddle.
"TOO wet!" he honks.

Jasper and Joop scurry to the
piggery. "Come play!" squeal
the piglets.

Jasper shakes his head.
Joop gleefully leaps into
the mud.

Jasper stares at Joop.
"Muddy mud," says Jasper.

Joop stares at Jasper.
"MUDDY mud!" honks Joop.

Jasper and Joop scamper to
the henhouse. "Come play!"
cheep the chicks.

Jasper shakes his head.
Joop rolls into the straw.

Jasper stares at Joop.
"Dusty straw," he says.

Joop stares at Jasper.
"DUSTY straw!" he honks.

Jasper and Joop scoot to
the beehive.
"Buzzzzzzzz!" warn the bees.

Jasper looks and listens.
Joop sticks his bill into
the beehive.

Jasper stares at Joop.
Joop stares at Jasper.

"RUN!" Jasper honks.

Jasper and Joop hide in the
grass. "RUN!" Jasper honks.

Jasper and Joop hide in the
mud. "RUN!" Joop honks.

Jasper and Joop run to
the pond.

SPLASH!
Jasper and Joop jump into
the pond.

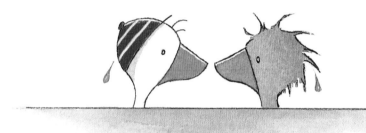

Jasper stares at Joop.
Joop stares at Jasper.

"What fun!" honk
Jasper and Joop.

Jasper laughs and flaps his wings. Joop stands on a rock and honks. They are best friends.